THIS BOOK BELONGS TO

Written by James Medd and illustrated by
Victoria Sawdon at bigfish® design limited

Printed in the UK

10 9 8 7 6 5 4 3 2 1

First printing April 2015

A E Rodda & Son
The Creamery
Scorrier
Redruth
Cornwall
TR16 5BU

ISBN 978-0-956967-3-4

Great Cream
Robbery takes
place HERE

Newquay

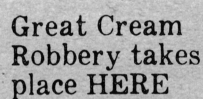

St Ives

CREAMERY

Truro

Penzance

Falmouth

Land's
End

Mousehole

Bude

Tintagel

Launceston

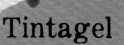

Bodmin

Liskeard

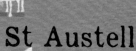

St Austell

Looe

THE GREAT
CREAM ROBBERY

James Medd & Victoria Sawdon

Merryn Malone was the cleverest cat
criminal in Cornwall. She had just finished
a very crafty theft, perhaps her best yet,
so she decided to take a well-earned day off.
The next day she would go looking for
an even bigger robbery.

She set off early the next morning. After hunting all day, she had found nothing.

Then, as it was growing dark, she smelled something really, truly, unbelievably delicious...

She followed her nose to a big blue building. Peeking in, she saw a room full of cows and in the middle, glowing like the sun, a bowl of clotted cream with a beautiful golden crust that looked better than anything she had ever seen, smelled or even dreamed of.

She had to have it.

Merryn went to sea to catch some fish and have a
good think. As she was looking back towards the
harbour, she saw a white flash. It zoomed down towards
the Pasty Shop, then it swung back up into the sky.

Merryn could see it was a bird, and it had a pasty
in its beak and two more in a bag round its neck.

She turned her boat around. She had found
her new partner in crime.

Merryn, being a clever cat, tracked down
the cheeky bird that evening. His name was
Blue, short for Blue Min, short for Bloomin'
Seagull. And yes, he definitely wanted
to be her partner.

All they needed now was a plan.
Down at Merryn's top-secret seaside den,
they began thinking very hard.

It didn't take Merryn long to work
out how they would get that cream.
As soon as it was dark, she clambered
onto Blue's back and he took off into
the night sky. Merryn guided him to
their destination, The Creamery.
When they were hovering above it,
she hopped off Blue's back and
parachuted elegantly down the chimney.

When Merryn reached the bottom, she almost jumped straight back out again. It was the middle of the night but there was a cow guarding the cream – a cow with one eye open. Merryn scrambled back up to the roof.

They were going to need an even cleverer plan.

They spent the next day cutting and sewing and measuring. When they had finished, they had their very own cunning cow costume. With both of them hidden inside, they would be able to walk straight into The Creamery, grab the cream and simply stroll away.

It might have worked too, if they had been just a bit better at cutting and sewing and measuring. Instead, they ended up in a muddy heap with their costumes in tatters. The cows sent them packing and back to the den they went.

Finally, after two whole days
of thinking and watching and
thinking again, they had it.

And this time it was a plan
that couldn't possibly, not in
a million years, go wrong.

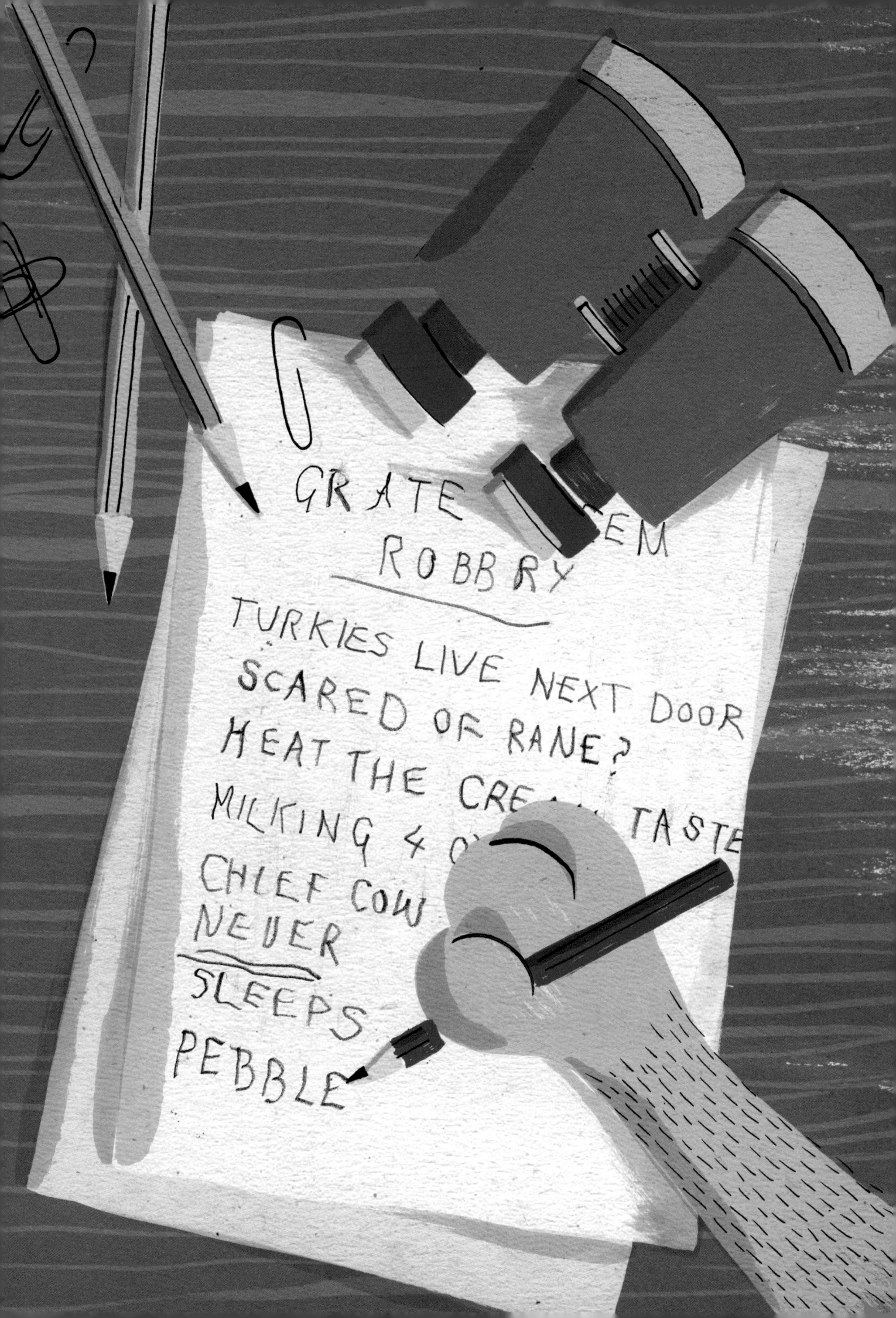
GRATE
EM
ROBBRY
TURKIES LIVE NEXT DOOR
SCARED OF RANE?
HEAT THE CRE
TASTE
MILKING 4 O
CHIEF COW
NEVER
SLEEPS
PEBBLE

The following morning,
they were in their positions
before the sun came up.

All was quiet.

CREAMERY

Merryn was hiding in the bushes. She gave
their secret signal: a purr, then a point,
then a paws-up. Blue took off, weighed down
by his bag and a bucket hanging from his beak.

The great cream robbery had begun.

Blue flew in low over
The Creamery, turned
on his side and tipped
his bag. Pebbles poured
out onto the roof.
**Plink plank
tucka tickum
tickum clack.**

Then, with a dainty
flip of his toe, he spilled
water from the bucket.
Sploof.

Inside, the cows were peacefully pouring and cooking and tasting.

When they heard the pebbles on the roof, they stopped still. It sounded like rain – and when it rained, like all cows, they had to go and lie in a field.

The water on the roof switched on their special Rain-O Meter. Alarms **boomed**. Lights **flashed**. That meant it absolutely had to be raining and Erica, the Chief Cow, had no choice. She told them all to **head for the fields immediately.**

RAIN-O METER

NASTY CLOUDS   JUST A SHOWER   LIE DOWN

WISHY WASHY   BEIGE   GORGEOUS GOLD

Meanwhile, Merryn had been busy outside.

In the field next door was a flock of
turkeys and she had just let them all out.

Like a chuckle-gobble-chattering train they streamed out of the field...

...and collided with the cows.
Feathers flew. Hooves clattered.
In all the mayhem, no one saw
Merryn and Blue slip into
The Creamery.

**Everything was going
exactly to plan.**

Except...

the delicious, rich cooking smell was wafting out of the open doors and windows of The Creamery. Now there were dozens of cats, all of them ready to try anything to get their paws on that clotted cream.

Every cat in Cornwall came running. They dived into the dishes, pounced on the pans and charged at the churns. Merryn and Blue could only watch as all that gorgeous clotted cream vanished in a blur of swishing tails and twitching whiskers.

Realising they'd been tricked, the cows returned
from the field. They found their kitchen full of
sleeping, purring, oh-so-happy, swollen-bellied cats
as well as one very cross Merryn and a baffled Blue.

Seeing all the trouble she'd caused, Merryn invited the cows to a giant cream tea picnic to say sorry.

She brought a huge pile of scones and lots of sweet strawberry jam and the cows came along with some of their delicious clotted cream. It was a feast they'd never forget and they became firm friends.

Then the cows had a big meeting. They talked
about the trick with the rain, and the turkeys,
and how much cats must love clotted cream.
They agreed that Merryn was a very clever cat,
and Blue Min was rather useful, for a seagull.

Erica had a brilliant idea. She asked her
new friends to come and help them at the
creamery. Merryn purred with pleasure
and Blue squawked in delight.

So Merryn gave up her life of crime for a **life of cream.**

And she never stole so much as a fish-tail again. **Well, that's what she said, anyway.**

HEAD TASTE